margaret Tempest.

THE
GREAT ADVENTURE
OF HARE

BY ALISON UTTLEY
PICTURES BY
MARGARET TEMPEST

LONDON: WILLIAM HEINEMANN LTD.

THE GREAT ADVENTURE OF HARE

IT WAS A LOVELY MIDSUMMER morning, and Hare looked out of his bedroom window on to the fields where cloud shadows were running races. Gentle blue butterflies and fierce little wasps flew among the flowers in the garden below. Hare stroked his whiskers and said "Just the day for my adventure."

"Grey Rabbit, Grey Rabbit, come here," he called over the banisters, "and bring my walking-stick, will you?"

A SCAMPER OF LITTLE FEET echoed on the brick floor in the kitchen, and Grey Rabbit ran upstairs with a cherrywood stick and a teazle brush. Hare took down his new blue coat from the hook behind the bedroom door. He put it on, with Grey Rabbit's help, twisting his head to get a good view of the two brass buttons at the back. Grey Rabbit brushed off some tiny specks of whitewash with her teazle. She had to stand on tip-toes to reach his shoulders, she was so small.

"ARE MY BUTTONS ALL RIGHT?" asked Hare.

"Yes, like two looking-glasses," replied Grey Rabbit, as she gave each one a rub with a duster, and then peeped at her face in the dazzling buttons.

"Don't forget your watch," she added, as the Hare started downstairs.

"OH DEAR, HOW CARELESS YOU are, Grey Rabbit," said the Hare, taking a large flat silver watch from the chest of drawers, and putting it in his waistcoat pocket. "I nearly went without it."

"Good-bye, Squirrel," called Hare, as Squirrel looked up from the mittens she was knitting. "Good-bye, I'm off on my great journey. Good-bye, Grey Rabbit, I shall be back for supper, and mind there is something nice."

He stepped out of the little door into the sunshine.

"TAKE CARE OF YOURSELF," cried Grey Rabbit, running after him and waving her paw. "Mind the traffic, and give Toad our present."

"Don't forget to bring a present back," called Squirrel.

He was going to visit the famous Toad who lived in the Ash Wood. Squirrel had laughed when he said he was going, and said, "You never dare."

"Darsen't I?" he said. "You'll see!"

Grey Rabbit decided to give the house a summer-cleaning whilst he was away. So Squirrel took her knitting up an apple-tree to be out of the way, and Little Grey Rabbit, with scrubbing brush and pail, prepared to clean the rooms.

HARE SHUT THE GARDEN GATE with a bang, and prepared to leap over the brook.

But he changed his mind, and sat down by the water, as a mocking voice cried, "Haven't you gone yet? You'll never get to Ash Wood if you don't start," and he saw Squirrel's face peering down from the apple-tree.

Hare marched off pretending not to hear.

Suddenly he bumped into a scared rabbit, who was looking behind him. Both fell head over heels but the rabbit picked himself up, and ran on.

A SOUND CAME FROM BEHIND A tree, and a Cock Pheasant walked out with proudly lifted legs.

"Good morning, Pheasant," said the Hare. "It's a fine day to-day. I've just had a tumble – some stupid rabbit, not looking where he was going."

"Hush," whispered the Pheasant.

"Why, what's the matter? Don't you live here?" asked Hare.

"No, my home is in the glade yonder," said the Pheasant, "but I don't want these fellows to know. Too many shady people in this wood. Only last week I had my water-butt emptied and my larder ransacked by a thief."

"Who was it, do you think?" asked Hare.

"It was Jay; he left a bit of his blue scarf behind him," and saying this, the Pheasant flew away with a heavy flap of his wings.

Hare ran on until he came to a great oak tree with a little door, and a silver bell hanging by a thin rope.

"Should I ring Moldy Warp's bell?" thought he. "Suppose Owl should come. What could I say? I'll ask the way to Ash Wood."

HE PULLED THE STRING, AND "Tinkle, tinkle" sang the tiny bell. Hare got ready to run, but a sleepy voice called, "What do you want, Hare?" and Owl looked out, blinking in the sunlight.

Hare faltered, "Er – er – er – which way is the way to Ash Wood, please, Wise Owl?"

The owl looked down severely, and Hare quickly got out his silk handkerchief from his coat pocket and waved it violently.

"What do you mean by waking me up for such a question? Where is your money?"

HARE STARTED, REMEMBERING how little Grey Rabbit had lost her tail; but Owl had seen his shining buttons.

"I'll take those buttons from the back of your coat," said he, and he clambered down, and cut them off.

"Go through the wood and the Teazle field, through the village, across the railway line, through Bilberry Wood, past Home Farm, and the Ash Wood is at the top of the hill," said the Owl, all in one breath. "A Fox lives in Bilberry Wood," called Wise Owl.

Hare turned pale. Owl had already climbed upstairs and shut the door.

OVERHEAD A LOUD SCREAMING laugh startled Hare, who stood undecided and alarmed. A blue Jay, who had been listening, flew by.

"Ha-ha! ha-ha! Frightened Hare! Timid Hare!" he mocked.

Hare grabbed his stick, straightened his shoulders, and began to whistle, "Rule, Britannia" which annoyed the Jay, and off he went.

"I expect the Fox won't notice me. I'm a pretty fast runner," said he.

He ran through the seeding blue-bells, and purple foxgloves flowering under the nut trees and great oaks.

He ran down the stony path, where ants laboured among the patches of yellow pimpernel, under the roof of beech and elm, to the gate at the end of the wood.

I N THE TEAZLE FIELD WERE RED butterflies gathering honey from the ragwort, brown bumble bees, eager to talk to anyone, busy hoverflies, with no time to spare, red-caped ladybirds, and field mice in bonnets and shawls, running on errands, strolling home, gossiping by the tiny green paths, playing on swings and roundabouts. It was such a busy world after the quiet wood. Hare walked across the field swinging his stick, feeling very important in his bright coat among all these little people.

THEY ALL KNEW LITTLE GREY Rabbit, for she got her teazle brushes here, and Hare answered many kind inquiries about her.

"Where are you going, stranger?" asked a Brown Rabbit.

"To Ash Wood, to visit Toad," answered Hare, pompously.

"My! You are a traveller!" exclaimed the Rabbit, admiringly.

"I am that," said Hare.

"What other countries have you seen?" inquired the Rabbit.

"Well—I've seen too many to tell you about. I'm a very famous Hare."

They pressed closer and stared at him with wide, innocent eyes.

"WILL YOU TELL US ABOUT ASH Wood and Toad when you come back?"

"That I will, if you meet me at half-past twelve."

"There's a fox in Bilberry wood," said a quiet little Hedgehog.

"I'm not afraid of a Fox," cried Hare.

He sat by the spring, put his two paws under his nose, and fell asleep.

He was awakened by the youngest Rabbit who tugged at his watch. Hare sprang up in a hurry; he had slept longer than he intended.

He left the field by a gap in the hedge, and ran through the village.

A TORTOISESHELL CAT ARCHED her back and spat at him, and a dog barked and tugged at his chain. A baby opened his eyes very wide, and pointed at him, and an old man fumbled in his pocket for his spectacles to stare at him.

He leapt the limestone wall, and crossed the field to the railway. The gleaming hot rails burnt his toes, and the roar of a distant train terrified him, as he scampered across and hid in the grass at the other side whilst the express rushed by.

"That's a Dragon," said he, mopping his head. "I must be in China. I *shall* have some adventures to talk about when I get home."

He climbed up a steep path into a rocky wood, "on the edge of the world," thought he.

Great cool spaces were about him, and a green roof above, held up by trees like pillars. The softest moss covered the rocks lying about on the ground, and bilberry bushes, jewelled with pink flowers, grew by the path. The sun shone through the lacy boughs and dappled his fur and blue coat with yellow circles. The air was so cold and fresh, like a drink of spring water.

"CAN YOU TELL ME THE TIME?" asked a silken voice, and Hare saw a fine gentleman in a red coat sitting on a fallen tree.

"Half-past twelve," said Hare, consulting his watch.

"Really? As early as that? Perhaps you would like to see my collection of birds' eggs?"

"Delighted," said Hare, who was flattered by this notice. "On my return. I am a bit of a collector myself. I collect Noughts and Crosses." and he trotted on, whilst the fine gentleman gazed longingly after him.

THERE WAS A CURIOUS SMELL which disturbed Hare. "It must be some foreign scent on his handkerchief," thought Hare.

He picked a branch of honeysuckle and twined it round his head, and held a sprig of marjoram to his nose, but the smell remained until he left the wood and crossed the fields to the stone farm on the high ridge.

Dappled cows stood under the trees, and a score of hens chattered excitedly about the Fox, who, the night before, had tried to open the hen-house door.

I N FRONT OF HIM LAY ASH WOOD.
Apple-green moths and honey-bees
came to meet him as he entered. The
flowers grew in groups, a patch of red
campion here, a clump of forget-me-nots
there, and tall bell-flowers, in their blues
and purples, like mists on the ground.

"Herbs for old Toad, I suppose," said
Hare to himself. "He does a lot of doc-
toring, they say."

In the middle of the wood was a bog,
and there, perched on an island, was a
small house with a roof thatched with
rushes.

"WHO'S THERE?" BOOMED A voice, as Hare waded through the bog with his coat-tails turned up.

"It's Hare, from Grey Rabbit's house, over the valley," said Hare.

The little door opened slowly and an immense Toad waddled out, leaning on a crutch. His eyes were bright as green lamps, and his cheeks were wrinkled with age. He wore a green coat and yellow breeches, old and creased, but Hare felt a shabby nobody when he looked at the wise animal.

"I have brought a present," said Hare, as the Toad gazed at him.

H E SEARCHED ALL HIS POCKETS, and then took off his coat. He looked in his waistcoat pockets, but it wasn't there.

The toad stood, whilst Hare turned everything inside out.

"Here it is," he cried at last. "Grey Rabbit stitched it inside my coat-lining." He cut the stitches and brought out an egg-beater.

"It's to beat eggs, you know, make them frothy," explained Hare.

Toad was entranced. He held it between his knees and turned the handle so that the wheels whizzed.

He whizzed it in a bowl of cream which stood on the door-step. The cream foamed in a whiteness.

"Butter," said he.

"Come in, come in, Hare," he cried, throwing open the little door. Hare walked through to a courtyard, where a fountain played.

Toad beat up the fountain and made rainbows of light.

Then he rang a hare-bell, and two frogs appeared.

"Bring refreshments for this gentleman," he commanded, "and a bowl of wood-pigeons' eggs."

THE FROGS RETURNED WITH saffron cake which Hare ate greedily. The Toad beat up the eggs, and made wonderful drinks which astonished Hare.

"I have no teeth," he explained. "It's a most useful gift, most useful. I have never been so pleased."

He took Hare to a cupboard which was crammed with odds and ends. There were skipping ropes, tin cans and ginger-beer bottles, mouth-organs, matches – all the things that picnickers had left behind.

"CHOOSE A PRESENT FOR YOUR-self, and one for each of your friends," said Toad, and Hare hunted to find something suitable.

He chose a tiny pair of slippers for Little Grey Rabbit, a boxwood flute for Squirrel, and a penknife with a corkscrew for himself.

Then Toad unlocked a secret drawer and took out a small bottle labelled VENOM.

"I shall give you a bottle of my famous Venom," said he, "But take great care of it. You had better give it to Grey Rabbit to put in the medicine cupboard."

HARE PUT IT IN HIS POCKET, with the slippers, flute and knife.

As Hare waded through the bog he turned round and saw the Toad busily beating the air with the egg-beater.

It was dusk when he ran across the fields to Bilberry Wood, and a little crescent moon hung in the sky.

"Hello!" said a voice. "You've been a long time," and Hare saw the red-coated gentleman sitting on a stile. At the same moment a strange odour came floating to him, and his heart fluttered and bumped against his side.

"Oh! Sir!" said he, "you quite startled me. I had forgotten about you."

"WHY, YOUNG FELLOW, I'VE been expecting you to supper," replied the Fox with a leer.

"I'm afraid it's too late, I'll put off my visit, if you don't mind," said the Hare.

"It's quite early, and really you *must* come, everything is ready," said the Fox.

They arrived at a ruined Mill house beside a stream. The Fox pushed Hare into the kitchen. Fox was an untidy animal. In a corner lay a gun, a trap, several snares, a jemmy for forcing doors, and a complete burglar's outfit.

HARE SAT UNEASILY ON THE edge of a stool, and Fox lay back on a broken rocking-chair.

On the table was a very large dish, as big as Hare, a plate, a long cruel knife and a pot of red-currant jelly.

Hare felt more and more uncomfortable. "I really must go," said he, as the stars blinked at him through the broken window, and a little wind moaned round the house. Was Grey Rabbit sitting up for him? Would the Squirrel miss him?

"Not yet, not yet. You've only just come," said the Fox. "Would you mind taking off your coat and weskit? They might fit a young friend of mine."

HARE GOT MORE AND MORE alarmed. He handed his lovely blue coat and waistcoat to the Fox, and a paper fell out of the pocket.

"Hello, what's this?" asked the Fox, and opened the paper covered with noughts and crosses.

"It's a game," stammered Hare.

"Let us play," said the Fox, and he drew his chair up to Hare's stool.

Fox learned quickly and beat him every time. Hare was too frightened to look what he was doing; his eyes were glancing round the room to find a way of escape. The door was locked, and the broken window gave the only chance.

"THAT'S ENOUGH," SAID THE FOX, putting the pencil and paper in his pocket, and he picked up the coat and turned out the pockets. He brought out the silk handkerchief, the ash twigs, a boot-lace, the little slippers, a marble, the flute, the Venom bottle.

"Hello? What have we here?" said he,

examining the small green bottle. "Scent? What? Scent? Conceited Hare to carry scent in your pocket!"

He took out the cork and poured some of the liquid on the silk handkerchief. Then he put it to his nose. His eyes closed, his ears drooped, and he sank with his head on the table, insensible.

HARE SPRANG UP, SEIZED THE half-empty bottle of Venom, cut the watch from the Fox's neck with his new knife, swept up the slippers, and the flute in his paw, and made for the window. He scrambled through, without waiting for his coat and stick, for already the Fox's eyes were rolling, and his legs kicking.

Away he ran through the wood, tumbling over stones, pitching into brambles, slipping, sliding, rolling down the slopes, his breath panting, his eyes starting.

AT FIRST HE HAD NO IDEA WHERE he was, but a glance at the stars showed him the way. He crossed the railway line, and ran through the edge of the village, where dim lights shone in the windows.

When he arrived at the spring he found four sleepy little Rabbits, and a Hedgehog, waiting for him.

"Here he comes, here he comes! Hurrah!" they cried. "What time is it? We've waited for ages."

"Half-past twelve," panted Hare, and he stopped a moment to breathe.

"YOU'VE BEEN A VERY LONG time," said the Hedgehog.

"I stopped to play noughts and crosses with Mr Fox," said Hare, and they all opened wide their mouths with astonishment. Then he hurried on, up the steep field to the wood.

"It's been wonderful to meet a real explorer," they said.

Hare clasped the bottle of Venom tightly in his paw as he went through the deep wood, ready for any Weasel or Stoat whom he might meet. As he ran out of the trees he saw a candle burning in the window of the little house, and he shouted for joy.

GREY RABBIT AND SQUIRREL heard him, and came running down the garden path.

"Oh, Hare, we thought you were dead, especially as Wise Owl told us there was a Fox in Bilberry Wood," they cried, as they clung to him.

"He caught me," confessed Hare, "and I only escaped through Toad's kind present to us all." He gave a shiver as he thought of the Bilberry Wood and smiling Mr Fox. They entered the house and Hare told his story, and put his presents on the table.

Squirrel tootled on the flute, and Little Grey Rabbit tried on the silver birch slippers, which fitted her as if they had been made for her small feet. The Venom she locked up in the medicine cupboard, among the stores of camomile, wormwood, and rue.

"I've had my great adventure," said Hare. "I am famous all over the world, and now I shall lead a quiet life at the fireside."

He wound up his watch, took his lighted candle, and went slowly upstairs to bed.

GREY RABBIT AND SQUIRREL looked at one another and laughed softly. Then they followed, and soon the only sounds in the house by the wood were the snores of Columbus Hare.

William Heinemann Ltd
Michelin House
81, Fulham Road, London SW3 6RB

LONDON · MELBOURNE · AUCKLAND

Text and illustrations copyright © William Heinemann 1931
First published 1931
This edition published 1992
ISBN 434 96928 1
Produced by Mandarin
Printed and bound in Hong Kong